The Lonely Daffodil

Story by Emily Langhorne

Illustrations by Heather Heyworth

"A great lesson for all, wrapped up in sweet words and beautiful illustrations."

—Jordan Chouteau, author of *No More Monsters Under Your Bed!*

"*The Lonely Daffodil* by Emily Langhorne is a touching story of longing and acceptance. The small daffodil at the edge of the forest is shunned by the ones on top of the hill. They have no use for his little voice, and he is lonely. When the daffodil witnesses a small kindness from a big tree to the tiny squirrel, he is curious. When the tree explains, the daffodil's heart blooms with understanding. During the spring, summer, and fall, the daffodil extends his kindness and makes many friends. After a long winter night, he awakes and finds himself with a surprise. This is a story about yearning, the power of kindness, and our connection with one another. This tale of a small daffodil at the edge of the forest is delightfully illustrated and gives the story a dreamy, magical feel."

—Kashmira Sheth, author of *Tiger in My Soup*

BELLE ISLE BOOKS
www.belleislebooks.com

ISBN: 978-1-953021-73-1

LCCN: 2022904614

Printed in the United States of America

Published by
Belle Isle Books (an imprint of Brandylane Publishers, Inc.)
5 S. 1st Street
Richmond, Virginia 23219

BELLE ISLE BOOKS
www.belleislebooks.com

belleislebooks.com | brandylanepublishers.com

To my mom, who shared with me her love of daffodils.
To my dad, who spotted the lonely one in the forest.

Dear Julian,

May your days
be filled with
wonderful stories

After the birds had flown south and before winter's first storm, the farmer went up the hill to plant the daffodils. She carefully placed each bulb in the ground—except for one.

The little bulb rolled out of the basket and down the hill and settled in a hole at the edge of the forest.

The days became shorter and the nights grew colder as winter slowly passed. All the while, the bulb slept peacefully. When the springtime sun began to shine, he awoke. It was not long before he grew into a sunny yellow daffodil.

He was bright, beautiful, and warm, but he was also alone.

At night, the daffodils on the hill sang together. He heard their songs and longed to join in, but when he asked them if he could, they laughed at him.

The other daffodils yelled, "Our songs are already beautiful. We don't need your little voice."

And the daffodil was lonely.

One day, the daffodil watched as a squirrel pulled acorns from a giant oak tree. The tree winced in pain, yet he did not protest. After the squirrel left, the daffodil asked the tree, "Why do you let him take your acorns if it hurts you?"

"Because he is the smallest squirrel," explained the tree. "The bigger squirrels collect the fallen acorns, leaving him none, and I should help him if I can, for he is smaller than I."

The following morning, after the wind had knocked acorns from the tree's branches, the daffodil gathered a pile beneath his leaves. The other squirrels came and went. When the smallest squirrel arrived, the daffodil uncovered the hidden acorns.

The tree thanked the daffodil for his kindness while the squirrel ate breakfast.

The daffodil asked the tree, "Will you sing with me tonight?"

"I'm sorry, but I cannot," said the tree. "I must talk with the trees. Without my voice, their stories would not be complete, but you and I are friends, and friends we shall remain."

The daffodil smiled. He had made a friend.

But the night came, and the songs of the daffodils echoed down the hill. The daffodil cried to them, "May I join your songs tonight?"

The others answered, "We have no use for a voice that talks with trees."

And the daffodil was lonely.

The next day, a cloud covered the sun. Rain began to fall. It fell faster and faster and frightened the daffodil, but the cloud above yelled, "Don't be afraid! Celebrate the rain! Dance and laugh with me!"

The daffodil danced with the raindrops. They slid down his stem and across his petals, and the cloud laughed with joy.

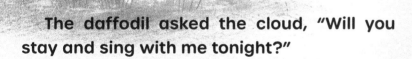

The daffodil asked the cloud, "Will you stay and sing with me tonight?"

"I can't, for I must go with the wind and celebrate the rain," said the cloud. "But I promise I'll see you again, my friend."

The daffodil waved cheerfully as the cloud drifted away. He had made a friend.

13

But the night came, and the songs of the daffodils echoed down the hill. The daffodil cried to them, "May I join your songs tonight?"

The others answered, "We have no room for a voice that laughs with clouds."

And the daffodil was lonely.

The next day, a bee flew into the forest and hovered near the daffodil. She said, "Little flower, I have flown a long way, and I am very tired. May I rest upon your petal?"

The daffodil nodded.

The bee napped in the warmth of the sun. When she awoke, she hummed her thanks. "I feel much better now," she said.

The daffodil asked the bee, "Will you stay and sing with me tonight?"

"I'm sorry, little friend, but I must buzz with the bees," she said. "Don't worry. I'll visit you again soon."

The daffodil happily hummed goodbye as the bee flew away. He had made a friend.

But the night came, and the songs of the daffodils echoed down the hill. The daffodil cried to them, "May I join your songs tonight?"

The others answered, "We have no place for a voice that hums with bees."

And the daffodil was lonely.

But the daffodil did not lose heart. He talked with the tree and played with the squirrel. He danced in the rain and hummed with the bees. He spent his days cheerfully, yet each night he listened longingly to the songs of the other daffodils.

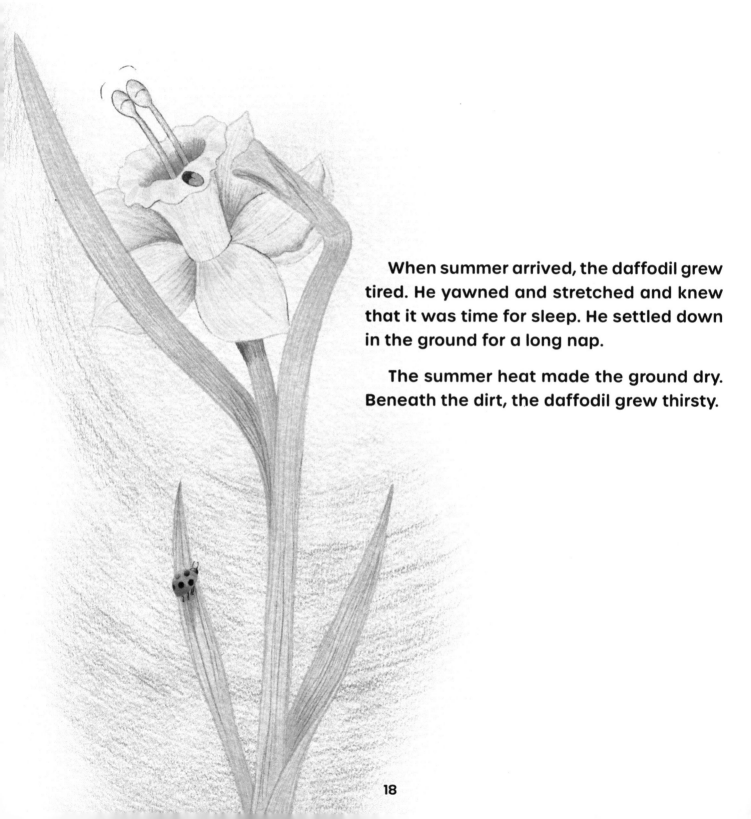

When summer arrived, the daffodil grew tired. He yawned and stretched and knew that it was time for sleep. He settled down in the ground for a long nap.

The summer heat made the ground dry. Beneath the dirt, the daffodil grew thirsty.

Thinking of his daffodil friend, the cloud drifted over the sleeping flower. Rain fell into the soil and trickled down to the daffodil's roots.

And the daffodil was no longer thirsty.

He slept deeply for a long time. Then winter drew near, and he began to shiver, for it was cold beneath the ground.

Remembering his friend's kindness, the oak tree leaned over where the daffodil slept and dropped the last of his leaves, blanketing the chilly flower.

And the daffodil was no longer cold.

When spring arrived, the daffodil awoke. The ground had warmed, and he knew it was time to get up, but he felt weak. Once above the ground, he began to wither. He was very sick.

But the daffodil was not alone, for his friend the bee had been awaiting his return. Nourishing him with the pollen given to her by flowers in a nearby field, she nursed him back to health.

And the daffodil was no longer sick.

Soon, the daffodil was again enjoying the company of his old friends. Just when he thought everything had returned to normal, the earth around him started to move.

Other flowers began to appear. Before long, the daffodil was surrounded by dozens of beautiful daffodils. Confused, he asked them, "How did you come to be here by the forest?"

A tall daffodil answered, "The farmer planted us here long ago, but we couldn't grow. The dirt was dry, and the ground was frosty. I was always too thirsty and cold to wake up."

Another daffodil added, "And those of us who tried to get up became sick because there were no bees here to help, so we went back to sleep."

The new daffodils beamed at him, and he returned their smiles with his own.

When night came, the daffodils by the edge of the forest sang together. Their voices traveled deep into the woods, where they were joined by the rustling of the trees, the humming of the bees, and the scurrying of the squirrels. The melodies made by the woodland's many different inhabitants created a beautiful harmony, and for the first time, all the creatures of the forest could enjoy the songs of the daffodils.

And the lonely daffodil was no longer lonely.

About the Author

Emily Langhorne lives in Dublin, Ireland. She grew up in Tidewater, Virginia (a region famous for its daffodils). Her writing has been featured in *The Washington Post*, *The Hill*, *Forbes*, and elsewhere. She loves sloths, traveling, being outdoors, playing bridge, and spending time with her husband. *The Lonely Daffodil* is her first picture book.

About the Illustrator

Heather Heyworth lives and works in a Suffolk market town in the UK. After graduating from Goldsmiths College, London University, she went on to become creative manager within a busy London design studio and then art editor at a large greeting card publisher. Her introduction into the world of children's books started with illustrating, designing, and co-publishing her own licensed character books. She wrote and illustrated her first picture book in 2009.

CPSIA information can be obtained
at www.ICGtesting.com
Printed in the USA
JSHW030728130822
29119JS00001BD/3